I Witness

The Taming of Roberta Parsley

By Carol Gorman
Illustrated by Ed Koehler

CPH™

SAINT LOUIS

To a gold-star teacher, Cindy McDonald!

I
Witness
Series

The Taming of Roberta Parsley
Brian's Footsteps
Million Dollar Winner
The Rumor

Copyright © 1994 by Carol Gorman
Published by Concordia Publishing House
3558 S. Jefferson Avenue, St. Louis, MO 63118-3968

Manufactured in the United States of America

Library of Congress Cataloging in Publication Data.
Gorman, Carol.
    The taming of Roberta Parsley/Carol Gorman.
      p.   cm.—(I witness)
    Summary: With kindness and Jesus' love, eleven-year-olds help "tame" the angry and rude new girl after she runs away from school.
    ISBN 0-570-04628-9 (perfectbound)
    [1. Christian life—Fiction. 2. Schools—Fiction. 3. Runaways—Fiction.]
I. Title. II. Series: Gorman, Carol. I witness.
PZ7.G6693Tam 1994
[Fic.]—dc20   93-388312

1 2 3 4 5 6 7 8 9 10   03 02 01 00 99 98   97   96   95 94

Contents

1

A Monster in School

I knew Roberta Parsley was a monster after just one day in school with her.

I don't mean the kind of monsters you see on cable TV. I'm talking about a mean, nasty person who makes people want to leave a room the minute she opens her big mouth.

Now, to be honest, I've been accused of having a big mouth myself. My dad, who's an English professor, says I'm *verbose, loquacious, and garrulous.*

But to be perfectly honest, I think I'm just a normal, intelligent, eleven-year-old girl who has a lot to say. A *lot.*

Anyway, I'll remember Roberta's first day at school for as long as I live. I'd never seen anyone like her.

Mrs. Pettyjohn, our teacher, introduced us to her just after she walked in the classroom door. She already had everybody's attention. Roberta is not someone you can ignore when you see her for the first time.

She was really tall, about a head taller than everyone else in the room. Her hair was long and stringy. She wore a cotton jumper and blouse that were about two sizes too big for her. They looked so wrinkled that I figured she'd slept in them the night before, and maybe the night before that too!

What I remember the most, though, was her face. She *sneered* at us. All of us. Everyone in my class had stopped working on their science projects. They stared at her.

"Everyone, this is Roberta Parsley," Mrs. Pettyjohn said.

She put her hands on Roberta's shoulders, but Roberta jerked away. She stared angrily over our heads at the back wall.

Mrs. Pettyjohn's smile faded a moment, then reappeared. "Roberta comes to us from the other side of the state. I'm sure you'll give her a warm Wilkin welcome."

The class didn't give her a warm Wilkin welcome. They didn't give her any kind of welcome. They just sat and stared at her.

Then Mike Fuller spoke up. "Where's she going to sit?"

There was a snicker at the side of the room. I didn't look over, but I knew it was Hilary Ralston.

"Not by me," she squealed, trying to stifle her laughter.

The kids looked over at her. Some of them laughed. They didn't want to sit by Roberta, either.

"Roberta," Mrs. Pettyjohn said, "there's an empty desk behind Juliet Hollingsworth. Why don't you sit there?"

So I was picked. I'm Juliet Hollingsworth.

My best friend, Tiffany Gallagher, turned around to look at me and rolled her eyes. I rolled my eyes back.

Why me? I thought. Why do I always get picked for stuff like this?

Last year in fourth grade, for instance, we had this kid in our class who was a little slow. Roseanne was her name. She spent some of the school day in another room and had art and music with us. She was okay most of the time, but sometimes she really flew off the handle. I mean, she could throw a temper tantrum any two-year-old could admire.

One day Mr. Hagerty, the art teacher, assigned us partners for a special project. It was a papier-mâché project, and all the work was going to be displayed around the room at Parent Night. With our *names* on them.

Guess who had to work with Roseanne.

Mr. Hagerty came up to me at the end of class. He pulled me aside and told me he had chosen me to work with Roseanne because I'm such a nice person. He said he was sure I'd be "sensitive" to Roseanne and her "needs."

I didn't say anything, but I was pretty steamed at first. This was my reward for being "nice"? I'd been hoping I could work with Tiffany.

Actually, though, it didn't turn out too bad. Roseanne didn't throw any fits, we got along pretty well, and I made up a fake name to put on our project. It was a papier-mâché horse, but it looked more like a cocker spaniel. Mr. Hagerty gave us an A for it anyway.

So now it was happening all over again. I was chosen to sit right in front of Roberta. I know Mrs. Pettyjohn planned it ahead of time, because up until today, there hadn't been an empty seat right behind mine. I sat at the back of my row.

Roberta trudged over to her desk, her heavy shoes *clunking* loudly all the way. She collapsed into her seat and shoved her feet out into the aisle. I couldn't help but notice that Roberta—how do I say this in a nice way?—Roberta didn't have the best smell in the world. In fact, she *reeked*. Abby Hart, who sat two desks over, made a face, coughed, turned a weird shade of gray, and held her nose.

Justin Talbot sat a seat across and one ahead of Roberta. He had watched her walk past him. He gazed at Roberta as if he were deep in thought. I think he was holding his breath, too, but I couldn't be sure.

Roberta looked across the aisle at him and scowled. Then she said in a low, gravelly voice, "What are *you* looking at, Dogface?"

Justin turned a bright strawberry red. Hilary exploded with laughter and kept it up until Mrs. Pettyjohn gave her a look that could've frozen Larkin's Pond solid in the middle of July.

"This is a lovely school, Roberta," Mrs. Pettyjohn said then, trying to muster a smile again. "And it's filled with lovely people. I think you'll really like it here once you get settled."

She glanced around the room. "Let's all sing the Wilkin School song for Roberta," she said, then turned to Roberta. "All the Wilkin students know the song. Pretty soon, you'll know it, too, and you'll feel more at home here."

Mrs. Pettyjohn sat down at the piano.

"Ready, everyone?"

The class sang:

Wilkin School, Wilkin School,
To you we all do sing.
We clap for you; we cheer for you.
Let the halls and rafters ring!
We're working hard; we're playing hard;
We do our best each day.
Here is where our friendships start
And never go away!

Mrs. Pettyjohn turned and smiled at Roberta. "There," she said. "That's your introduction to Wilkin School. I hope you'll be happy here."

Roberta just scowled.

Then Mrs. Pettyjohn told the class to start working again on the science projects. She was big on projects. That was one of the things I liked about her. I like projects too.

We were studying ecology, and I was drawing some of the birds that live in the rain forests in Central and South America. Most of them were beautiful with brilliant, colorful feathers. I was using my favorite box of colored markers.

Mrs. Pettyjohn came back and talked to Roberta. She first kneeled down to talk. But then I think the smell got to her, and she stood up and backed off a little.

"We're almost finished with our science projects, Roberta," she said. She talked in a low voice so she wouldn't disturb the kids who were working. "It's probably too late for you to complete a project now, so why don't you take a stroll around the classroom? Each student will explain his or her project to you."

She took another step back. "Everyone," she announced, raising her voice, "Roberta will be walking up and down the aisles. Please tell her about the project you're working on as she goes by."

Mrs. Pettyjohn took a couple of quick steps to the window and opened it.

"It's a little stuffy in here," she murmured.

Everyone knew the real reason she had opened the window. Roberta was stinking up the room. Hilary laughed again and her friends, Stacy Wilson and Candy Miller, giggled and looked over at her.

Roberta hadn't moved yet from her seat. I didn't really want to turn around and look at her again, but I could see her a little if I turned my head and looked out the corner of my eye.

Roberta sat slumped in her seat, her arms folded across her desk.

"Roberta?" said Mrs. Pettyjohn, after opening two more windows. "Would you like to walk around and see everyone's project?"

Roberta made a disgusted, huffy noise and hoisted herself to her feet. "Why don't you start with Juliet?" Mrs. Pettyjohn said. "She has a beautiful bird project."

Roberta made a face. "Who's *Juliet?*" She said my name as if it tasted bad in her mouth.

"That's me," I said, turning around. "I'm not crazy about my name, either. My father's an English professor, and he named his kids after characters in Shakespeare's plays. I'm Juliet, my sisters are Portia and Cordelia, and our dog is Mercutio."

I'd told that story so often I could recite it in my sleep. Usually people laugh, or at least smile, when they hear it and make some remark about how clever my father is.

"Your father sounds stupid," Roberta said.

What I wanted to do right then was punch Roberta's lights out. But what I did was hold up my picture of birds.

"This is a barred ant shrike," I said, pointing to the small black and white bird with the dark plume on its forehead. "And this is a scarlet ibis. It's almost two feet long. And this is my favorite, the keelbilled toucan."

"If I couldn't draw any better than that," Roberta said, "I'd *quit.*"

I dropped the picture on my desk and stared at her. "If I couldn't be any nicer than you are," I said,

"I'd jump off the side of a mountain because no one would want to be my friend."

"Girls, girls!" said Mrs. Pettyjohn in her sternest voice. "We will not have that kind of talk in this classroom."

I wanted to point out that Roberta had started the whole thing by insulting my name, my father, and my drawing. But I didn't.

Mrs. Pettyjohn told Roberta to sit down. I guess she didn't want to risk her insulting any of the other kids' projects.

For the rest of the day Roberta slumped at her desk. At recess she sat alone behind a bush at the far end of the playground. At lunch she sat by herself at the end of one of the long lunchroom tables.

She didn't make any friends.

At the end of the day while all the kids were walking out of the classroom, Mrs. Pettyjohn smiled at Roberta. "I hope you had a pleasant day, Roberta," she said.

"It stunk," she said.

There was a scream of laughter from Hilary Ralston, who was about to walk into the hall. She turned back and grinned at Roberta. "It didn't stink as bad as you!" she shrieked.

Something told me this was going to be a long year.

2

Gold Apples

Roberta Parsley wore the same oversized jumper on her second day too.

She and I hadn't spoken to each other since the argument yesterday. I decided maybe I should think of something to say. Not something nice—I couldn't bring myself to go that far. Just something neutral that would show her I wasn't holding a grudge.

I didn't have time to think of anything. About ten o'clock, after a bathroom break, Tiffany and I were standing at my locker, talking. Roberta's locker was right next to mine, and I was leaning against the edge of her locker. She walked up and gave me a hard shove.

I staggered sideways. A strong whiff of Roberta filled my nose.

"Hey!" I cried. "What's the idea, Roberta?"

"'*What's the idea, Roberta?*'" she mimicked in a high voice. Then she said in her naturally low, gravelly voice, "You were in my way, *Jerk-i-et*."

"I wasn't trying to block you! All you had to do was ask me to move And my name is *Juli*et."

Roberta opened her locker, threw in a worn jacket, slammed the door, and stalked away.

"Do you think she's older than we are?" Tiffany asked. She stared after Roberta thoughtfully. "She's really big! Like a moose. Or an elephant." She laughed.

"Maybe she flunked a grade," I said.

Tiff nodded. "What a moron." Hilary Ralston appeared with Stacy Wilson and Candy Miller.

"I saw Big Roberta over here," Hilary said. She rolled her eyes. "Doesn't she have any other clothes? What a mess!"

"Doesn't she ever wash her hair?" said Stacy.

Hilary laughed. "I'd wear a bag over my head if I looked like that!"

"Well, maybe she can't afford to buy new clothes . . . " I started to say. But the bell rang, and Hilary and her friends squealed and ran for the classroom door.

Tiff and I went into the classroom too.

"This is Friday," said Mrs. Pettyjohn, starting class. She wrote the date on the board and the word *Friday*. "Who received gold apples this week?"

Most of the kids raised their hands.

Mrs. Pettyjohn smiled. "Very good," she said.

I guess I'd better tell you about the gold apples. It's a thing Mrs. Pettyjohn started in her class about a hundred years ago. When someone does something nice for you, or gets a good grade on a test, or something like that, you're supposed to give that person a gold apple. Mrs. Pettyjohn says it's kind of like a pat on the back.

She supplied us all with boxes of gold apples at the beginning of the year. They're really stickers of gold-colored apples. Before you give someone a sticker, you write a word or two on it that tells the reason why you're giving it to him or her. Some kids have them plastered all over their spirals and bookbags.

"The idea," Mrs. Pettyjohn said, "is to give them away. *Look* for people who do good things. A gold apple is a kind of reward. Give someone a pat on the back every day."

"But what if no one *deserves* it?" Hilary had asked. "What if nobody has done anything nice?"

"I'm sure," said Mrs. Pettyjohn, "that you'll find someone who deserves one, Hilary. You just have to look around you."

At first I wasn't sure who I should give apples to, either. But the second day after Mrs. Pettyjohn explained about the apples, Brit Malone, who sits next to me, helped me work out a hard math problem. When I finally understood the problem—math is my worst subject—I gave Brit a gold apple. I wrote on it, *Thanks for math help.*

She really loved it. I can still remember the look on her face. A big smile broke out over her face, and she said, *"Tha-a-nk you, Jul-i-et!"* as if I'd given her a sack of money or something. She peeled away the paper on the back and stuck it on her math notebook. It's still there, two months later. So I got the hang of it, giving gold apples to people in my class. And I got some too.

Mrs. Pettyjohn always likes it when a lot of people get gold apples. I guess she thinks her "Gold Apple Program," as she calls it, is a success.

"Justin," she said, "how many did you get this week?"

"Three," he said.

"Good," Mrs. Pettyjohn said, smiling. She wrote a 3 next to Justin's name. "Adam?"

"Two."

"Good. How about you, Brit?"

"Eleven," Brit said and blushed.

Brit gets tons of gold apples every week because she's always doing stuff for other people.

"How about you, Juliet?" Mrs. Pettyjohn asked.

"Two," I said. Two had seemed pretty good until Brit said she'd gotten eleven.

"Great," said Mrs. Pettyjohn.

She went through the rest of the class and marked the numbers on the board.

"Since Roberta has only been here for a day," Mrs. Pettyjohn said, "I won't even ask her. But I'm sure that by next Friday, she'll have a couple of apples too."

"*She's kidding!*" Hilary whispered to the girl next to her.

Mrs. Pettyjohn pretended not to hear. "I think we had a very positive week," she said. "There were a lot of good things going on here."

"Mrs. Pettyjohn," said Hilary, raising her hand. "I think some people are just giving gold apples to their friends and not looking outside of their cliques."

"Why do you say that, Hilary?" Mrs. Pettyjohn asked.

"Well, I only got two apples this week," Hilary said. "And I only got two apples last week. And both times, they came from my friends." She didn't say *Stacy* and *Candy* but she didn't have to. Those two girls were probably the only kids who'd even *consider* giving Hilary a gold apple. The rest of the kids would have wanted to give her a punch in the mouth, most likely.

"Hilary may have a point here," Mrs. Pettyjohn said. "Folks, I think you should look hard this week to find good things about classmates you haven't given an apple to yet."

"Of course, they have to *deserve* them," Hilary said.

"If you look hard, you'll find reasons to give apples to everyone in the class," Mrs. Pettyjohn said.

"*Everyone?*" Hilary asked Mrs. Pettyjohn. A little smile crept across her face. She nodded meaningfully back toward Roberta.

"*Everyone*, Hilary," Mrs. Pettyjohn said firmly.

"Eeooooo," Hilary exclaimed, wrinkling her nose.

Hilary wasn't very nice about Roberta. But, I couldn't think how Roberta was ever going to earn gold apples either. She was just too nasty.

I felt a stab of guilt. We're always hearing in Sunday school that you should love and help everyone. I guess I knew that included Roberta too. Jesus loved her. But how could I?

I didn't look behind me to see whether Roberta had realized that Hilary was talking about her.

But I found out later that day because Roberta paid her back. Big time.

We were at lunch. Tiffany and I eat together at a table in the middle of the lunchroom. (The lunchroom is really the gym. The custodians move in big tables after the morning gym classes.) Roberta was sitting by herself at the end of a table not too far from us.

Tiff and I were almost finished eating when Hilary walked over with Stacy and Candy. She held something in a napkin.

"Would either of you like my brownie?" Hilary asked us.

"Yeah!" I spoke up fast. Brownies are my favorite food.

Hilary dropped it on my plate.

"There you go, Juliet," she said. "I don't eat things with a lot of calories anymore. I want to stay looking nice and slender. So I thought *you* might like it."

I looked at Tiffany and rolled my eyes. "Gee, thanks, Hilary," I said.

"Enjoy," she said. She twiddled her fingers in the air, then turned and strolled away.

"She wants a gold apple," Tiffany whispered over the table at me.

I knew that already. Why else would she do something nice?

I glanced over at Hilary, and I saw what was going to happen an instant before it happened.

Hilary turned to say something to Stacy and didn't see that Roberta sat just a few feet away.

With one quick move, Roberta slipped her foot in front of Hilary. Hilary's toe caught on Roberta's ankle, and she went flying head first to the floor, her arms and legs sprawling out to the sides, and—this is the worst part—her skirt flew up to her waist.

Some of the kids in the cafeteria screamed, I suppose either out of embarrassment for Hilary or fear that she'd hurt herself.

Roberta doubled over her lunch; she was laughing so hard.

Stacy quickly pulled down Hilary's skirt.

Hilary turned bright red, her eyes wide with fury as she slowly raised herself up from the floor.

Mr. Hagerty, who supervised in the lunchroom, came running from the other side of the room.

Hilary began yelling, "She *tripped* me! She *tripped* me!" and pointed to Roberta.

Mr. Hagerty pulled Roberta up from her table. "Come with me, young lady," he said.

Roberta was still laughing. Mr. Hagerty hauled her away from the table and out of the cafeteria.

3

Thief!

W hat's on tap for today, Juliet?" my mom asked. "That is, after you've cleaned your room?"

She stood at the kitchen counter and poured pancake batter onto the electric griddle in perfect little round disks. My dad leaned over with his head in the refrigerator. I think he was looking for the orange juice.

"The mall," I said. "Can I clean my room when I get back? I didn't mess it up much this week."

"Good," Mom said. "Then it won't take you long to clean it. You can go to the mall right after it's picked up and clean."

"But I promised Tiffany that I'd meet her in front of the fountain at ten," I argued. "I think Melissa and Abby are going to be there too."

Mom sighed and glanced over at Dad, who was still rooting around in the fridge.

"Then call Tiffany and tell her you're going to be a bit late," she said. "Find Portia and Cordelia, will you, Juliet? The pancakes are about ready."

"Where are they?" I asked.

"I don't know," she said. "That's why I said *find* them."

"Can't find the juice, honey," my dad said.

"It's behind the milk jug," Mom said.

I ran upstairs to find my sisters. Portia and Cordelia were in their room, sitting on their beds. They're seven years old and identical twins.

"Breakfast is ready," I announced.

"I'm not hungry," Portia said. "Why do we have to have—"

"—pancakes every Saturday?" Cordelia said, finishing the sentence. Portia and Cordelia often finish each other's sentences.

"I don't know," I said. "Ask Mom."

"I'd rather have oatmeal," said Cordelia.

"With lots of sugar and raisins," said Portia.

The girls followed me downstairs.

"Since we can't have oatmeal for breakfast, can we go to a movie tonight?" Cordelia asked as we walked into the kitchen. Cordelia liked to bargain.

"Not tonight, honey," Dad said. "I have a stack of papers to read. We'll try it next weekend."

"We never get our way," Portia complained.

23

"Juliet," my mom said, "you're going to the mall. Why don't you rent a movie for tonight?"

"YEAH!" my sisters cried in unison.

"Okay," I said. "How about *Rock and Roll Vampires from Outer Space*? Melissa said it was good." I sat in my chair at the round kitchen table.

"YEAH!" the girls yelled, jumping and bouncing around on the floor. "*Rock and Roll Vampires*! Yeah!" They stopped jumping and looked at each other.

"Dad, what's a vampire?" Cordelia asked.

Mom motioned us to the table. "That movie doesn't sound appropriate for young children," she said. "Girls, sit down."

"How about a nature film?" my dad suggested, sitting at his seat. "A good old-fashioned family movie?"

"Well," I said, "there's *Forest Fury*."

"What's that about?" Mom asked.

"It's about a crazy guy who goes through the forest setting fires and—"

"Yeah!" my sisters yelled. "*Forest Fury*!"

"*Juliet!*" my mom said.

"Dad wanted a nature film," I said.

"That's not what I had in mind," my dad said.

"Choose a movie that's good for young children!" Mom said. "What about *Bambi*?"

"Are you kidding?" I said. "I can't rent that at the mall! What if some of the kids from school are there?"

My parents looked at each other. They obviously didn't get it.

"Mom, Dad," I said, as patiently as I could, "I'm eleven-and-a-half years old. In only eighteen months, I'll be a teenager. I need to start practicing."

"Practicing what?" my dad asked.

"Being cool!" I said. "Teenagers would never rent *Bambi*. It's just not cool."

Mom stared at me a moment. "Something tells me your teenage years aren't going to be easy."

"Don't worry, Mom," I said. "I'll be okay."

"I'm not worried about you!" she said. "I'm wondering if *I'll* survive them." Dad laughed.

Anyway, just before we said grace, I promised I'd rent *Bambi* if I got the chance, when none of the other kids were around to see me.

When I got to the mall, Tiffany was sitting at a table with Melissa Brown and Abby Hart. Soda cans littered the table, and a large cardboard envelope of fries sat in front of Tiffany.

"Looks good, Tiff," I said, sliding into the fourth chair.

"Yeah," she said, munching away. "Soda and fries—I love 'em. What a great breakfast!"

Melissa leaned in. "Guess who we saw a few minutes ago?"

"Who?" I said.

"The big R.," Melissa said. "Roberta Lettuce."

"You mean, Roberta Parsley?" I said.

Melissa's face turned pink. She shrugged. "Yeah. Same difference. You know who I mean."

"Where was she?" I asked.

She jerked her head. "Over by Alexandra's."

Alexandra's is a store with girls' clothes.

"I hope she buys something!" Tiffany said. "She sure needs some new clothes."

"She sure does!" said Abby.

"Do you think she'll take a bath tonight?" asked Melissa.

"Who knows?" said Abby.

"I hope so!" said Tiffany. "I don't think I can stand to smell her anymore!"

"You sit right in front of her," Abby said to me. "Do you hold your breath a lot?"

"Sometimes," I said. "Mostly, I just hope she doesn't act like a jerk."

"You sure told her off the other day," said Melissa.

"I liked it when you said you'd jump off a mountain if you were like her!" said Abby.

"Me too," said Tiffany, grinning.

Something happened when they said that. Somehow it didn't sound very nice. Roberta started the fight, but did I have to get back at her?

"That was fun to watch," Melissa said.

I changed the topic. "Want to go to the Sports Arena?"

"Why would you want to go there?" asked Melissa. "They only have sports stuff."

"I want to look at a new catcher's mitt."

Melissa rolled her eyes. "Are you kidding?" she said. "I want to look at clothes."

"Want to come with me?" I asked Tiffany.

"Uhm, I'll meet you at Alexandra's," said Tiffany. She smiled. I think she was hoping I wouldn't be mad.

I wasn't mad. In fact, I was hoping she wouldn't want to go. I wasn't really going to the Sports Arena, even though I would like a new catcher's mitt. I was going to duck into the video store and pick up *Bambi*. I'd brought my backpack so I could stuff it in there as soon as I'd rented it.

I told Tiff, Melissa, and Abby that I'd meet them in a little while.

Video Village was halfway down the mall corridor. To get there I had to pass Aldren's, a big department store. As I walked by the entrance, I glanced inside. There were a lot of people milling around.

They were looking at shoes and jeans and belts and blouses.

I'd just about passed the door when I spotted Roberta Parsley. She said a few words to a woman who looked just like her, only a lot older. I suppose she was Roberta's mother.

Then the woman-who-was-probably-Roberta's mom turned and walked over to the saleswoman.

And that's when I saw it.

Roberta whipped a pair of jeans and a shirt off of their hangers and stuffed them into a big shopping bag.

I stopped dead in my tracks and stared at her, my heart pounding hard. I don't know why I was surprised to find out about Roberta, but I was.

Roberta Parsley was a thief.

4

Thou Shalt Not Steal

I didn't want to stand in the entrance to Aldren's Department Store any longer. I didn't want Roberta to see me and guess that I'd watched her shoplift.

I moved along, staring at the floor, until I got to the Sweet Tooth. I wandered in, vaguely aware of the chocolate aroma in the air.

Roberta Parsley, shoplifter.

I'd never known a shoplifter before. It felt funny knowing Roberta Parsley could have been arrested for what she'd done. So could her mother.

Her mother. Her mother must have known what Roberta did. In fact, didn't her mother keep the saleswoman busy while Roberta did the stealing? Did they *plan* it that way?

"May I help you?"

I looked up to see a large woman standing behind the counter. She stared at me.

"I was just looking," I said.

I left the store and walked back toward Alexandra's. Then I remembered I was supposed to get *Bambi* at the video store, so I doubled back.

I picked up the movie and headed again toward Alexandra's to meet Tiff and Melissa and Abby. When I passed Aldren's, I kept my eyes straight ahead so I wouldn't be able to see Roberta if she was still there.

I'd already decided that I'd tell Tiffany, but no one else. I *had* to talk to someone, but it had to be someone I could trust. Someone who wouldn't spread it all over school that I'd seen Roberta shoplift.

I could trust Tiffany. And I could trust God too. Lord, I breathed, help me handle this the right way.

I found the girls in front of Alexandra's.

"Let's see your catcher's mitt," said Tiffany, grabbing the sack from my hand. She peeked inside. "You got a movie?" She pulled it out of the sack.

Rats. I'd forgotten to put the movie into my backpack. I'd been thinking about Roberta.

"Bambi?"

I'd blown it. What could I say? Now they were going to laugh.

"Yeah, well, I don't really—" I started to say.

"I *love Bambi!*" said Tiffany.

"Oh, me too!" cried Abby.

"Except when his mother dies," Melissa said. "That always makes me cry."

"Don't you love Thumper?" Tiffany said.

"Yeah!" I said. I smiled a little grimly. If God could get me through the *Bambi* episode, maybe He'd help me with Roberta too.

We talked about *Bambi* for a while, then spent the rest of the afternoon wandering around the mall. I bought a pair of earrings, and Melissa bought a pair of jeans on sale at Aldren's. I kept my head down in case Roberta and her mother were still there. I didn't think they would have hung around, but I didn't want to take the chance that I'd see them.

I hoped I could get Tiffany alone so we could talk, but it never worked out because Melissa and Abby stuck to us like glue.

Finally, Melissa and Abby said they had to go.

Good, I thought, now I can tell Tiff.

I told her on the bus while riding home. We sat on the seat in the back, away from the other riders. I whispered the whole story to Tiffany.

"You *saw* Roberta steal clothes from Aldren's?" Tiffany said, her eyes wide.

I nodded. "Her mother distracted the saleswoman so she could do it."

"Her mother *helped* her?" Tiffany said. "What are you going to do?"

"What do you mean?" I said.

"Are you going to turn her in to the police?" Tiffany asked. "Or are you going to tell Mrs. Pettyjohn? Or your parents?"

"Do you think I should?" I asked. I really didn't know what to do.

"Maybe," Tiffany said. "This is big news. I mean, this is really *BIG NEWS!*"

"I know," I said. "But don't tell anyone, okay? At least, not now."

"How come?" Tiffany said. She looked disappointed.

"Because I don't want it getting around," I said.

"Why?" Tiffany said. "You, yourself, yelled at her for insulting your drawing."

"I know," I said. "I can't stand Roberta. In fact, I kind of hate her. She's mean. But I just don't want everybody to know what she did."

"But if you hate her—"

"You know when I said I wouldn't want to be like her?" I said.

"During your fight at school?" Tiff asked.

"Yeah," I said. "Well, when I said I'd jump off a mountain, it didn't make me feel better."

"It didn't?" Tiffany said. "I thought it was funny."

"Yeah," I said, "but, well—I don't know." I thought a minute. How could I explain this without sounding like a nerd? "Look, Tiff, you know I go to church. Jesus didn't go around hating people and being mean to them. When you and Melissa and Abby were laughing about what I said to her, I guess I didn't feel I was following His example."

"She deserved it!" said Tiffany. "She said mean things about you— and your *dad!*"

"I know," I said. "But I think she would've said those things about anyone." I stared out the bus window a minute before I spoke again. "So don't tell anyone about her shoplifting, okay? I want to think about it first."

"Okay," she said. "Suit yourself. But I'd tell everybody if I were you."

I spent a lot of time thinking about Roberta Parsley that night. I pictured her in my mind, with her stringy hair; her wrinkled, too-large jumper; her angry face.

And I thought about her mother. Her *mother* who helped her shoplift. That's what I couldn't get over.

I couldn't imagine Mom helping me do something illegal. She wouldn't even call the school and say I was sick that time when Tiff and I got back so late from our families' camping trip the night before. Tiffany's mother did. Tiff got to sleep till eleven that day. I had to go to school because my mother wouldn't tell a little lie for me.

But Roberta's mother helped her *shoplift*. Maybe she even *taught* her how to do it.

That made me sorry for Roberta. Even though she was a creep. I closed my eyes and asked God, again, for some help.

Life sure can get complicated.

The next day was Sunday and my family went to church as usual. Pastor Lekvoldt talked about how God gave Moses the ten commandments on Mount Sinai. He said that the commandments are just as important today as they were in the time of Moses.

Then he read the commandments from the Bible.

I listened to the first seven commandments. It was the seventh that roared like thunder in my ears: *Thou shalt not steal.*

That sentence echoed in my head for the rest of the sermon and through the next hymn. I thought about Roberta. And I thought about God. I wondered if God would punish Roberta for breaking the Seventh Commandment. I figured God was pretty serious about His commandments.

I suppose Roberta deserved some kind of punishment. But our Sunday school teachers have always talked to us about how God forgives us our sins. That's why Jesus died on the cross for us.

But don't we have to be sorry for doing bad things before God forgives us?

I bet Roberta wasn't the *least* bit sorry.

I wondered if I should tell on Roberta. That way she would get punished and maybe learn that she shouldn't steal.

I wondered if that would make God happy.

The thought of turning Roberta in just didn't feel right to me. Somehow I had the feeling that it *wouldn't* make God happy. Maybe God would find another way to teach Roberta. I decided to keep my mouth shut about what I'd seen at the mall.

What I didn't know was that the story about Roberta had already spread like wildfire.

Everyone already knew that Roberta was a thief.

5

Tiffany's Big Mouth

I heard it first on the playground just after I got to school on Monday morning.

"*Juliet!*" It was Melissa's voice. I can always tell when Melissa is yelling at me. She has a screechy kind of sound when she's excited.

I looked in the direction from which the screech had come. Melissa was huddled with Abby and Hilary and Stacy on the sidewalk leading up to the front door to the school.

"Did you hear the *news?*" Melissa cried. She broke away from the group and scurried toward me, waving her arms wildly around her head.

"What news?" I asked.

"You didn't *hear?*" she gasped. She glanced over her shoulder at the others and waved them to come over. She turned back to me. "It's about Roberta Lettuce!"

"Parsley," I said.

"Whatever," she said. "Roberta's a thief! She shoplifted some stuff from Aldren's."

"What?" I said. *How could she know this?*

"It's true!" Melissa said.

Hilary, Abby, and Stacy ran over.

Hilary put her hands on her hips. "First she trips me in front of the whole school and *laughs* about it; then she shoplifts clothes from the mall! I suppose next we'll hear she's *murdered* somebody!"

"How do you know Roberta shoplifted at the mall?" I asked.

"Tiffany told us!" Melissa said. "She saw the whole thing!"

"She *did?*" My heart started beating hard.

"She told us all about it!" Stacy said.

"And get this," Melissa said. "Her *mother* created a division—"

"A what?" I said.

"I think it's a 'diversion,' " Hilary said.

"Well, her mother talked to the salesperson so Roberta could steal without her getting caught," said Melissa.

"Tiffany told you this?" I said. I could feel a hot, tingling sensation in my cheeks. "She *saw* everything that happened?"

"Yeah!" said Melissa.

Just then, out the corner of my eye, I saw a familiar red sweater. I turned and saw Tiffany. Her smile faded when she saw me, and she started walking away fast.

"*Tiffany!*" I yelled at her.

She stopped and turned.

"You have the biggest mouth this side of the Mississippi, do you know that?" I hollered at her.

Melissa, Abby, Hilary, and Stacy stared at me as if I'd gone crazy. Tiffany's face turned as red as her sweater.

"I thought I could *trust* you!" I yelled. "I thought I could tell you a secret, and you'd *keep* it. You know why I thought that? Because we're supposed to be *best friends*, that's why! And you know what? I don't want you for my best friend anymore! What do you think about *that?*"

I turned around and walked up the steps and into the school. I walked to my locker, threw my stuff inside, and slammed it shut.

I heard a little noise down the hall. I looked up and saw Roberta, led by a serious looking Mrs. Arnstead, walking down the hall.

Mrs. Arnstead is the principal.

Roberta was in trouble. I figured it was probably because of her tripping Hilary at lunch on Friday. I figured Mrs. Arnstead couldn't arrest Roberta for shoplifting at the mall. So it *had* to be the tripping incident.

I turned and walked to the girls' bathroom and opened the door. "Hey, Juliet!"

It was Megan Wheeler. She sits two kids ahead of me in my row. She was standing at the edge of one of the sinks, drying her hands on a paper towel.

"Did you hear about Roberta?" she said. She was grinning as if she had a great story to tell me.

"What?" I asked. I knew, but I asked anyway.

"She shoplifted some junk from Aldren's over the weekend," Megan said.

"Yeah," I said. "I heard."

"I wish she'd gotten caught," Megan said. "People shouldn't be able to get away with stuff like that."

"I bet she wears her *new* clothes to school today," she said.

"Maybe," I said. I couldn't remember what Roberta had been wearing in the hall just now. I wished Megan would go away. I wanted some time by myself to think.

Megan continued to babble. "Tiffany Gallagher saw the whole thing. She stood right there in Aldren's and *watched* while Roberta stole those clothes!"

I was so mad at Tiffany. She'd told me she wouldn't tell about Roberta! Now it was all over school, and Tiff hadn't even seen what had happened!

Tiffany was becoming a celebrity. And I didn't like it.

I'd wanted to do the right thing and not tell anybody. But now that everybody knew, shouldn't they know that *I* was the person who saw everything?

The first bell rang. It was time to go to the fifth-grade classroom. Megan was still yakking as we walked to the classroom.

I didn't look at Tiffany.

"Okay, folks," said Mrs. Pettyjohn, "please get seated. There's something I want to talk about with you."

We all moved to our seats and sat down.

"I assume that you all heard what happened in the cafeteria on Friday," Mrs. P. said.

"Boy, did we," said Melissa.

"Roberta *laughed* about tripping me!" Hilary cried.

"I know," said Mrs. Pettyjohn. "We don't need to discuss the incident any more. I wanted you to know that Roberta has been placed on in-school suspension today for what she did to Hilary."

"Only one day?" Hilary exploded. "That's all? She should've gotten *expelled* or something!"

"Hilary, I know she embarrassed you and made you angry," Mrs. Pettyjohn said. "I don't blame you a bit. But Mrs. Arnstead met with Roberta and her mother on Friday afternoon and decided that one day of in-school suspension would be just punishment."

"Mrs. Pettyjohn," said Melissa, "Roberta and her mother are shoplifters. Tiffany saw them both taking stuff from Aldren's Department Store."

Mrs. Pettyjohn turned to Tiffany. "You actually *saw* Roberta stealing?" she asked.

Tiffany glanced at me out the corner of her eye. She looked at the top of her desk and nodded.

"She took a pair of jeans and a shirt," said Melissa. "Her mother was in on it. She talked to the saleswoman so Roberta wouldn't get caught!"

"Roberta wasn't caught?" Mrs. Pettyjohn said.

"Nope," said Melissa.

Mrs. Pettyjohn frowned. "This is very serious." She turned and walked slowly to her desk. Then she turned to face us.

"Well," she said, "I think maybe that tells us something about Roberta's life at home. She isn't getting the right kind of direction, apparently. And, you know, she may not be getting enough love."

"Who could love Roberta?" Hilary said. She laughed, and so did Stacy and Candy and some of the other kids.

I had to admit I agreed. Roberta would be pretty hard to even *like*.

"She's such a jerk," Hilary said. "If people hate her, it's *her* fault!"

"Well, her behavior is certainly part of her problem," Mrs. Pettyjohn agreed. "But I want you to think back to last Thursday, Roberta's first day here at Wilkin School. Do you remember when she first walked in here?"

"How could we forget?" said Melissa, laughing. "She looked like a freak!"

Hilary nodded. "Her hair looked so oily and stringy. And it still is! Yuck!"

Mrs. Pettyjohn nodded. "And what do you think your faces looked like to Roberta when she walked in here?"

The class became silent for a moment.

I said, "I think we looked shocked. She wasn't like any of us."

"That's right," Mrs. Pettyjohn said. "How do you think she felt when she saw your faces?"

"Bad," said Justin.

"Yes," said Mrs. Pettyjohn. "And that's sad because Roberta is your classmate."

"She's mean!" Hilary said. "She *tripped* me and then laughed!"

"She *does* do mean things," Mrs. P. said. "But maybe she saw your faces and knew after hearing a few of you laugh at her"—Mrs. Pettyjohn looked directly at Hilary—"that she wasn't going to be welcome here. Maybe she decided to show you first that she didn't care."

"Is that why she stole the stuff from the mall?" asked Stacy.

"I don't know why she may have shoplifted," said Mrs. Pettyjohn. "Maybe she wanted some clothes so she could fit in better here at school." She stood and looked around the classroom at us. "Do you know the power you people have?"

"Power?" said Abby.

"That's right," said Mrs. Pettyjohn. "You have the power to make Roberta miserable or happy here at school."

"She doesn't *want* to be happy!" Hilary said.

"Everyone wants to be happy," Mrs. P. said.

"How could we make Roberta happy?" asked Brit.

"By giving her attention, the right kind of attention," Mrs. Pettyjohn said. "By complimenting her when she does something good and giving her a gold apple, or just by smiling and showing her a friendly face when she walks by."

"She'd probably spit on my shoes or something," said Melissa.

"I guarantee she wouldn't do that," Mrs. Pettyjohn said. "Roberta wants friends just as much as anybody else."

"So what do we do if she does something mean?" Hilary asked. "What if she calls us names? What do we do then?"

"Nothing," said Mrs. Pettyjohn.

"*What!*" Hilary cried. "*Nothing? We stand there and take it?*"

"You can walk away," said Mrs. Pettyjohn. "But don't answer back."

This all sounded kind of familiar.

Then I remembered why. One morning a couple of months before, my Sunday school teacher had talked about "turning the other cheek." None of the kids in my Sunday school class thought they could do it either. We all agreed that if someone were screaming mean things at us, it would be very hard to turn away and not yell back something just as mean.

"You see," said Mrs. Pettyjohn, "what Roberta wants is your attention. If you don't *give* her attention when she's mean, she won't get what she wants."

"I feel kind of sneaky," Brit said. "I mean, talking like this behind Roberta's back."

"I'm going to talk with Roberta today before she leaves school," said Mrs. Pettyjohn. "I'm going to tell her what we've talked about. I'll tell her that we all want her to have a good year and that we're going to help her with her behavior."

"She'll be mad," said Melissa.

Mrs. Pettyjohn nodded. "She may be very suspicious at first. But as soon as she sees that you all are sincere about wanting her to have a good year, I'm sure she'll change her mind."

She stopped and looked around the room at us. "Well," she said, "are you with me? I know you can do it. Are you ready to give it a try?"

Brit spoke up first. "This'll be fun!" she said.

"This'll be hard," said Melissa.

"Maybe," said Mrs. Pettyjohn, "but I know you all can do it. I want you to know that I think this is a *very* special group of kids. I couldn't ask every class I've had to do this."

I could see that nobody really wanted to be nice to Roberta. It would be very hard not to get mad when she was mean. But, I figured, it might be a good experiment.

"We might as well give it a shot," I said. I sent another prayer to God. He'd really have to help me with *this*.

"Okay," said Melissa grudgingly. "I guess I could try it for a while."

There were nods around the room and a few groans, but I think everybody decided it was worth a try.

As hard as it seemed, we were going to try and tame a monster!

6

Turning the Other Cheek

I was a little nervous when I got to school the next day. I'd never turned the other cheek as far as I could remember. I thought it was probably going to be very, very hard.

I wasn't too worried about the part where we give Roberta a smile or gold apple for being nice. I figured Roberta couldn't *possibly* be nice, so we'd never have to do it.

I wasn't too anxious to see Tiffany, either. I wasn't as mad as yesterday, but I didn't feel like being friendly yet. A promise is a promise, and best friends are supposed to keep their promises.

I threw my stuff into my locker and turned around just in time to see Mrs. Pettyjohn walking into the classroom with Roberta.

Roberta was wearing a new pair of jeans and a yellow T-shirt—the same clothes I saw her steal from Aldren's Department Store two days ago.

I followed them in.

The kids in the room suddenly got very quiet. Everybody stared at Roberta in her new clothes. They all looked at one another with big eyes and nodded. They knew she was wearing stolen goods.

"Good morning, everyone," Mrs. Pettyjohn said cheerfully. "I see you're all ready to begin."

She came around to the front of her desk, and Roberta sat in her seat.

"Just so we start with everything out in the open, I talked with Roberta yesterday afternoon. I told her that we're going to help her have a good year. She agreed to our plan; so we'll start this morning. Okay?"

One voice answered.

"Okay," Brit said. She turned around and smiled at Roberta, who didn't even look up.

Mrs. Pettyjohn cleared her throat. "Today I'm going to tell you about a new project in social studies. We've been studying the pioneers for the past several weeks. I think you've enjoyed it, haven't you?"

The kids were still thinking about Roberta. Some of them were turned in their seats staring at her. But a couple of kids nodded at the teacher, answering her question.

Mrs. Pettyjohn smiled. "Good. Now, instead of taking a test on this unit, you're going to work in teams on projects to present to the class."

"Like what kind of projects?" asked Melissa, turning back to the front of the room.

"There are many possibilities," said Mrs. Pettyjohn. "You could do a report on the major trails that the pioneers took to get to the West. Or you could research what they ate and possibly bring in some home-cooked examples to share with the class. That kind of thing. What do you think?"

"It's a *great* idea!" I said. As I said, I love projects. Roberta was already pushed into a corner of my mind.

"And no test!" Melissa called out.

Everybody liked the no-test part the best.

"The projects will be due in two weeks," said Mrs. Pettyjohn. "I have a list here of possible projects." She passed sheets down the rows. "If you have other ideas to add to this list, let me know."

"You'll work with others on this project," Mrs. Pettyjohn continued, "so go ahead and choose your groups, two to four students in each group."

There was a lot of talking, then, while everybody decided whom they'd work with. I sat there, trying to decide what to do. Usually, I work with Tiffany. *Should I ask her to be in my group?* Even though I was a little bit mad, I'd still rather work with her than anybody else.

I looked at her. She was peeking at me out of the corner of her eye.

"Be in my group?" I mouthed the words.

Tiffany beamed and nodded yes. It made me feel good.

Brit hurried over to me from the front of the room. "Could I work with you, Juliet?" she said.

"Sure," I said. "Tiffany's in our group too."

Tiffany came over and sat down across the aisle from me in the seat that Justin had just left to join his group. Brit sat behind Tiffany in the last seat.

Roberta, just behind me, sat alone, staring down at her desk. Then she opened the top of her desk and stuck her head inside. She rummaged around in the papers and notebooks, looking busy. I think she was hoping nobody would notice she wasn't making plans with anybody.

Mrs. Pettyjohn approached us.

"Brit, Juliet, Tiffany," she said, "could Roberta join your group? I don't think she's hooked up with anyone yet."

"Sure," Brit said before I could give her a signal not to agree.

Tiffany looked at me with horror in her eyes. "But—" she started to say, "—uh, Mrs. Pettyjohn, we already have three people, and—"

"You may have up to four," Mrs. Pettyjohn said. "Thank you, all three of you."

She looked over at Roberta, who was still pawing through the inside of her desk. "Roberta, will you please join these girls for the project?"

Roberta lowered the desk lid enough to look over the top, and she scowled.

"We'll have fun," said Brit, smiling. Tiffany made a face.

Roberta dropped the top of the desk. It fell with a loud *THUD*. She slammed her arms down on the desk and grunted.

I decided to ignore her. After all, wasn't that part of turning the other cheek?

"So what do you guys want to do for our project?" I asked.

Tiffany looked at the sheet our teacher had passed to us. "How about a skit? It says here we can do one. But—" She looked at Roberta and back at me. "Maybe a skit wouldn't be such a great idea."

"Yeah!" Brit said. "A skit sounds like fun."

"Okay," I said. I like skits. Maybe we could give Roberta a tiny part so she wouldn't mess it up too much.

"Really?" Tiffany said. "Are you *sure?*" She kept giving little nods of her head toward Roberta. "Maybe we should do something else."

"Do you have any ideas, Roberta?" Brit asked.

"*No,*" Roberta growled, staring at the wall.

"Well," Brit said brightly, "let's all brainstorm together."

Tiffany, Brit, and I talked for awhile and decided we could be four women making the journey from Missouri to the Oregon country.

"Oh, this'll be *fun!*" Brit said, beaming. "We can make costumes—I *love* to sew—and we'll do some research about everyday life."

"One of us can be the mother," I said. "Our father has died, and we want to start a new life in a new land."

"That's wonderful!" Brit said.

Tiffany nodded. "Roberta should be the mother because she's so much bigger than the rest of us."

"Shut up, you ugly witch!" Roberta barked at her.

Tiffany's mouth opened in surprise. Then her eyes narrowed, and her mouth turned down at the corners. Tiffany was really, really mad. And Tiffany doesn't turn the other cheek very easily.

I knew it then. This was going to be the worst project any of us had ever done.

7

Meeting with Roberta

Y ou think she'll show up?" Tiffany asked.

She stood in my living room, looking out the front window.

It was Thursday after school. We were meeting at my house to work on our social studies project. Roberta hadn't arrived yet.

"She'll come," Brit said. She stood next to Tiffany and looked out at the street.

"She'd better not come," Tiffany said. "I don't know if I can stand being in the same room with her."

"You'll be fine," Brit said shortly. "There, see? There she is now! I told you she'd come." She pointed down the sidewalk.

"She's still wearing those clothes she shoplifted," Tiffany said. "She wore them all week, the thief."

"Maybe she doesn't have anything else besides those clothes and the cotton jumper," I said.

"So what?" Tiffany said.

"Let's forget about her clothes," Brit said. "Let's give her a chance."

Tiffany rolled her eyes and sighed loudly. I went to the front door and pulled it open.

"Hi, Roberta," I said.

She stood on the large wooden front porch. She stared at her feet. Her stringy hair fell away from her face.

"Come on in!" said Brit, who had just come up behind me.

I opened the door wider and she walked inside. She stood in the entryway and looked into the living room. She seemed to be taking in everything: the bookcases along the far wall filled with Mom's books, the TV set with the VCR on top, the coffee table in front of the couch, the big stone fireplace with the oak mantle over it.

I led Roberta into the living room. "Mom picks up my sisters about 4:30 at the sitter's, so they'll be here pretty soon."

Roberta didn't say anything, but sat on the end of the couch as far away from us as she could get.

"I had an idea last night about our skit," Brit said. "How about this? The scene is a quiet evening in a cabin built in the Oregon country. The sisters and mother are fixing supper and talking about what they did that day—you know, about all their chores and everything."

"That sounds good," I said.

Tiffany didn't respond. Neither did Roberta.

"What do you think, Roberta?" Brit asked her.

"I don't care," Roberta said, scowling.

"That's what I like," Tiffany said. "Enthusiasm."

Roberta turned to Tiffany and raised her fist. "You want to *fight* me, girl?"

Tiffany looked startled. She started to open her mouth.

"Okay," I said quickly, "let's make a list of the things these pioneers will talk about."

"They'd talk about the weather," said Brit brightly, "especially because of their crops and live-stock."

"They'd talk about tools that need repairing," I said.

"And fences that need mending," Brit said.

"These are liberated women," I said and laughed, hoping the others would laugh too.

They didn't. Roberta and Tiffany were still glaring at each other.

"What else would they talk about?" Brit asked Roberta.

"This is boring," Roberta said.

Tiffany glared at her. "What do you mean, boring?"

"Don't you know the word *boring?*" Roberta growled. "What an idiot."

"Who's an idiot?" Tiffany cried.

"What's boring?" I said.

"Talking about the weather," Roberta said, "and tools and fences."

Brit thought a moment. "Maybe Roberta's right," she said. "Maybe the skit will be boring."

"You have any better ideas?" Tiffany challenged Roberta.

"A *dance!*" Brit said suddenly. "Let's say there's been a cabin-raising that day. The cabin is all finished, and the women are preparing for the dance. They can talk about the new cabin and what food they've fixed—"

"Yeah," I said, "that's more interesting."

"Roberta!" Brit said. "This was a good idea! I think this will be much more interesting than sitting around talking about the weather! You were right! Weather is boring."

Roberta, not sure how she'd deserved Brit's compliments exactly, nodded, but said nothing.

The front door flew open. Mom, Portia, and Cordelia came in, everybody talking at once.

I introduced Roberta to Mom and the girls.

"Say," Mom said, "I'm going to make a big pot of turtle bean chili for supper. Would you three girls like to stay and share it with us?"

"Sure," Tiffany said.

"Thanks anyway, Mrs. Hollingsworth," Brit said, "but my aunt is coming to dinner at my house tonight."

"How about you, Roberta?" my mother said. "Can you stay?"

Roberta jerked her head around to stare at my mother. She looked amazed. But there was something else.

Was it terror?

She shook her head. "Can't," she said. Her voice was trembling. Why would she be scared to stay for dinner?

"Okay," Mom said cheerfully. "Maybe some other time." She left for the kitchen.

"Cord and I'll be out in the playhouse," Portia said.

She and Cordelia headed for the back door.

"I know!" said Brit, turning to me. "Since you and Tiffany like to write, why don't you guys write the script? Roberta and I can make the costumes. My mom has lots of old fabric we can use. Then we'll put it all together sometime next week."

"Great," I said. Tiffany nodded. I knew she was just as glad as I was that we wouldn't have to work with Roberta for a few days.

"Okay with you, Roberta?" Brit asked.

"Yeah, I don't care," Roberta said quietly.

"Juliet," Brit said, turning to me, "I didn't know you have a playhouse. Could we see it?"

"Sure," I said. "C'mon."

I led Brit, Roberta, and Tiffany out to the back yard.

"There it is," I said.

The little house was built by a carpenter who owned our house before we bought it. It stood about six feet tall, and it had a red roof and burgundy shutters. The door was small; an adult would have to bend over to step inside.

"It's *beautiful!*" Brit said. "Let's go inside."

"Knock first!" yelled Cordelia from the only window. She'd seen us coming.

Brit knocked on the front door, which was opened by Cordelia.

"What a *nice surprise!*" Cordelia said, using her best manners. "Please come in!"

We stepped across the tile floor. The house was empty as usual, except for the crunch of our six bodies.

"We're having tea," said Portia.

"No we're not; we're having espresso," said Cordelia. She held an imaginary pot. "Would you like a cup?"

"It's *tea*, Cordelia," Portia said sternly.

"No, espresso."

"Seen enough?" I asked Brit. I wanted to get out of there. When my sisters start arguing, you never know how long they'll be at it.

"You even have curtains on the windows!" Brit said. "It's perfect!"

"It was fun when I was a child," I said. I didn't want them to get the idea that I play house in it now.

Brit oohed and ahhed some more. Roberta stood there, looking around her, but she didn't say anything.

"I'd better get home now," Brit said. "Thanks for showing us your playhouse, you guys."

Portia and Cordelia had stopped arguing about what they were drinking. They nodded at Brit.

"Come back and see us again," Portia said, her good manners returning.

"Oh, yes. Very, very soon," said Cordelia.

"Come on, Roberta," said Brit. "I'll walk down the sidewalk with you a little way. We can plan when we'll get together and sew."

"See you guys," Brit called. She and Roberta headed around the side of the house while Brit chattered away about fabric and patterns.

"Roberta's such a jerk," Tiffany mumbled.

I watched Brit and Roberta walk away. Roberta sure was a strange person. But today I understood why she got so mad at Tiffany. Tiff had made that comment about her size. That's what started it all. Roberta was probably self-conscious about being bigger than everybody else.

But she didn't have to call Tiffany names.

I still didn't like Roberta. But today she didn't seem exactly like a monster. She seemed angry, but human.

Brit was trying to do what Mrs. P. had suggested. She acted as if she didn't notice Roberta's temper. And she complimented her on steering us away from talking about the weather in our skit. In fact, she gave Roberta the credit when *she* was the person who had come up with the good idea.

Maybe there was something to this turning the other cheek. And giving compliments. God's love does work miracles.

Maybe it could even tame Roberta Parsley.

Who's That Girl?

The next day when Mrs. Pettyjohn asked who earned gold apples during the week, a new hand went up.

"Roberta? Terrific!" Mrs. Pettyjohn said. "How many?"

"One," she said.

"Great," said Mrs. Pettyjohn.

Brit must have given it to her.

I glanced back at Roberta and smiled at her. She didn't smile back, but she nodded.

"Because of Roberta," piped up Brit Malone, "our social studies project is going to be really good!"

"Wonderful!" said Mrs. Pettyjohn. "We'll look forward to seeing it."

I wished Brit hadn't said that. Now everybody was going to expect big things. They might be disappointed. Tiff and I had better work really hard on that script.

We did work hard on Saturday and Sunday, and by the time the four of us got together again on Monday after school, the script was ready.

"Wait till you see Roberta in her costume," said Brit, grinning. She had just come downstairs from the bathroom where she'd been working on Roberta's hair. "She came over twice during the weekend, and we worked on costumes. Hers is the only one that's finished, but the others are close."

In a few minutes, we heard steps coming down the stairs. I looked up and gasped as Roberta walked into the room.

Brit grinned. "What'd I tell you?"

I gazed at Roberta for maybe thirty seconds before my mouth would work. I mean, she didn't even look like Roberta. She looked—well, she looked *pretty.* I could hardly tell it was the same person.

Brit had changed Roberta's hair. I'd noticed at school today that her hair was clean for the first time. But for the skit, Brit had pinned Roberta's hair up on top of her head. All of it didn't stay there, though, and little wisps hung loose around her face, which was nice.

The dress was really great. There was something familiar about it, but I couldn't put my finger on it. It was mostly white with little blue and yellow flowers printed on it. The collar was white and the dress buttoned down the front. The dress was gathered in little tucks at the waist, and the skirt was full and loose.

But maybe what was *most* different was Roberta, herself. She must have known how good she looked in the costume. She was smiling a soft little smile that I'd never seen before. It's amazing how a nice smile can make a hard, crabby face look pretty. She first looked at Brit, then Tiffany, then me.

I finally was able to talk.

"Roberta," I said. "You look—you look—*beautiful.*"

Roberta blushed and looked at the floor.

"Thanks," she said so softly I could barely hear her.

Then I realized why the dress looked so familiar.

"Are those your dining room drapes?" I asked Brit, pointing to the dress.

Brit laughed. "Yeah. My mom made the drapes, and there was some extra left over. She gave us the fabric and helped us a little."

"You look great, Roberta," said Tiffany. She said it grudgingly, but she said it. Roberta gave Tiffany a surprised look, then stared at the floor again.

"You're going to steal the show," I said. "Nobody will look at anyone else in the front of the class."

"I wouldn't blame them," Roberta said. She grinned.

I stared at her for a second, and then it hit me: *Roberta had made a joke!* I started to laugh, and Brit joined in, along with Roberta. Even Tiffany laughed. It was great to see Roberta laugh. Her face got rosy and her eyes shone. I could see by the look on Brit's face that she felt good seeing Roberta happy too. I think even Tiffany was glad to see Roberta laughing.

Then I handed everybody a script, and we read through it, each of us taking a part. When Roberta read her speech, we all looked up from our scripts to watch her.

" 'Have you seen the decorations for the barn dance?' " she read. "I walked down there this morning, and it looks so lovely, all decked out in red and yellow streamers. This dance is going to be the best thing that's happened to us since we arrived here!' "

I was amazed. Roberta really read well. I mean, she sounded like an actress you'd see in a movie or something. Her voice was normally low and kind of gruff, but when she read, the gruffness kind of faded out, and she had a softer, lighter sound.

"That was terrific!" Brit said when Roberta was finished. "Roberta, you might become a famous actress."

We all looked at Roberta with a little more respect and a whole lot more amazement.

Roberta nodded a little, accepting the compliment while she stared at the floor.

The rest of the read-through went pretty well.

"Let's work again on Monday after school," I said. "Try to have your lines memorized by then."

Brit, Roberta, Tiff, and I worked every day after school that week on our social studies project, and it was really going well. We had all our lines memorized on Tuesday, and the costumes were finished on Wednesday, so we had the rest of the week to polish the skit.

Best of all, the four of us were getting along pretty well. Tiffany was obviously trying not to cross Roberta, and Roberta left her alone. We each gave Roberta a gold apple for her great acting, and she seemed kind of happy to get them, saying, "Thanks," in a little voice while she looked at the floor.

Our group was scheduled to present our skit on Tuesday of the next week.

On Monday, the first day of presentations, we were all in our seats when the bell rang. We were curious to see the other groups' projects and compare them to our own.

First up was Adam Wheaton and Ross Hunter, who had drawn pictures and collected some old items that would have been taken on the long journey in a wagon train.

Their project was pretty good. Adam talked about the weapons the pioneers needed, such as rifles, pistols, gunpowder, lead, powder horns, and holsters. He had a picture of each thing he talked about, and he even brought an old bullet pouch that had belonged to his great-great grandfather.

Ross told us about the food people took with them. Flour, bacon, rice, tea, baking soda, coffee, corn meal, dried beans, beef, fruit, salt, and sugar were all necessary staples on the trip West.

It was a good project, but I thought ours was better, and that made me feel really good. I was getting a little itchy to show our skit to the class.

Then it was Hilary's turn. Of course, she was working with Stacy and Candy. She strode to the front of the classroom and flipped her long hair behind her shoulders.

"We have a very special presentation," Hilary said. "We're going to show you the *fashion styles* of the pioneers."

I sat up. This sounded more interesting than pioneer weapons and food.

"The women on the wagon trains were practical," Hilary said, "but *everyone* wants to look their best, so even these women dressed for fashion."

She unrolled her large sheet of paper. On it were drawings by Hilary, Stacy, and Candy. Hilary pointed to the first figure, a woman. She was standing next to a tree.

"Here is Elizabeth enjoying a moment of peace in the shade," Hilary said. "She's wearing a cotton gingham dress with a high collar and little white buttons down the front and decorative bric-a-brac around the yoke. Her sun bonnet shields her face from the sun. Back then, the women didn't *want* tans. It was very *in* to have pale faces."

Stacy pointed to a picture of a man. "This is Jake," she said. "Jake is the scout for the wagon train. He's in love with Elizabeth" (she pointed back to the woman figure) "and wants to look good for her when he rides back to the camp after seven days without a shower. So he wears a brown cotton shirt that won't show the dirt and sweat stains, and buckskin pants that never wrinkle, even after long days in the saddle."

It went on, with each new character either in love with somebody or trying to kill somebody else. Sort of a soap opera on the range.

It was kind of dumb, I guess, but it kept everybody's attention.

"Girls, that was very—interesting," Mrs. Pettyjohn said with a smile when it was over.

Our class took a break then, and we were excused to use the restrooms and the drinking fountains.

Brit approached Tiffany and me with a big smile. "Those projects were pretty good, but ours is even better," she said. She looked over my shoulder. "Roberta! Come here!"

Roberta walked over to us. She was wearing that wrinkled jumper and cotton blouse that she wore nearly every day when she first arrived. Lately she'd been switching back and forth between that and her stolen clothes. Her hair was still hardly ever combed, but she'd been keeping it cleaner these days. And she was smiling more often—maybe twice a week.

"Did you like Hilary's group?" Brit asked Roberta.

"It was dumb," she said.

"It was funny but kind of stupid," said Tiffany.

"*Really stupid!*" Roberta said. She laughed.

"I'm surprised that the pioneers were interested in fashion," Brit said. "I thought it was a struggle for them just to stay alive."

"Yeah," I said, "but it was entertaining."

"Our skit is entertaining *and* educational," Brit said.

I looked up then to see Hilary standing just behind Brit. She had heard everything we'd said about her group.

She looked mad.

"Well, *we* really want to see *your* project," she said. "We especially want to see Big Roberta here do her stuff."

Roberta's face got very red very fast. She took a step toward Hilary. "Our group will be better than yours, witch. Just wait and see."

Instead of getting flustered by Roberta's insult, Hilary pulled herself up straight, flashed a mean smile, and said, "Roberta, I wouldn't call anyone names if I were you. Have you looked into a mirror lately? Why don't you do something about that stringy hair of yours? And that wrinkled sack of a dress? And while you're at it, why not order yourself up another mother? One who doesn't *shoplift* with you. I hear you and your mom live in a crummy apartment over on Hay Street where she sits around getting *drunk* all day!"

There was a horrible silence then, while Hilary smiled wickedly, and everyone else stood there shocked and speechless.

Roberta's mouth had opened a little while Hilary was talking. Now her eyes filled with tears, and she turned and ran down the hall.

I felt a tremendous rush of anger stream through my body. We'd worked so hard with Roberta. She was getting along; she was even smiling sometimes. And now Hilary had ruined everything.

I whirled around to face Hilary.

"Why did you do that?" I yelled. "Why did you say those things? She didn't deserve that! Do you think she can help where she lives or what her mother does?"

"You had no right to say those things!" Brit said.

"You owe Roberta a big apology!" growled Tiffany.

Hilary took a step back, surprised that anyone was mad at her.

"Hey, I thought you all hated Roberta!" she said. *"She's* the mean one! She started it! She deserved what I gave her!"

"She was doing just fine with our group," I said. "She was even *nice.*"

I turned to Brit and Tiffany. "Come on," I said. "Let's go find Roberta."

We ran to the end of the hall, but we didn't see her.

"You check the bathroom," I said to Brit. "And Tiffany, check the gym. I'll run down to the primary wing."

We split up and headed our separate ways. I asked some little kids, probably first graders, if they'd seen a tall fifth-grade girl walking down here. They shook their heads no.

Brit and Tiffany returned to report that they hadn't found Roberta either.

"She must have left school," I said.

"Oh, Roberta, Roberta!" Brit said, putting her head in her hands.

"Where do you think she went?" Tiffany asked.

"I don't know," I said. "But I'm going to find out."

9

Where Is Roberta?

I pulled out the piece of paper from my pocket and checked the address we'd been given at the principal's office after school.

"This is it," I said. "1424 Hay Street."

The four of us huddled across the street and stared at the large brick apartment building looming up in front of us. Most of the windows were shaded, as if the people inside didn't want to let in the sunshine or face the world. Some of the bricks around the door were crumbling. The wooden front porch was sagging.

"Hilary was really mean about Roberta," I said. "But she was right about one thing. This place is crummy." I looked at Tiff and Brit. "What are we going to say when we see her?"

"I think we should tell her how we feel," Brit said.

We crossed the street and walked up the crumbling sidewalk to the front porch. I pulled open the heavy door, and we stepped inside.

The entrance was small and dark. A flight of stairs, led up into gray shadows. A row of mailboxes lined the wall to the right.

"There it is," Brit said, pointing to the box with *334* over it.

A little slip of paper, torn nearly in half and taped to the black mailbox, said *Parsley* in scrawled little letters.

"Let's go," I said.

We started up the stairs and puffed our way to the third floor. The hallway was covered with threadbare carpet, so dirty you couldn't tell what color it was.

We could hear loud music blaring from a radio someplace down the hall. We made our way along the corridor, past five heavy wooden doors until we got to 334. The loud music was coming from inside the Parsleys' apartment.

"Why doesn't she turn the radio down?" Brit asked.

"Think she'll hear us knock?" Tiff said.

"Go ahead," I said. Tiffany knocked.

The radio kept playing loudly. There was no other sound from the apartment.

I knocked this time, louder. Still no answer.

Then I yelled, "Roberta!"

Then we all knocked on the door at the same time and yelled "Roberta!" at the same time.

"She *had* to have heard that!" I said.

Suddenly, the door across the hall was yanked open, and an old man in a dirty bathrobe stood in his doorway, glaring at us.

"S'bad enough I gotta listen to that music all day," he yelled at us. "Now some fool kids'er screamin' their heads off out in the hall. Quiet down, ya hear me! Or I'll call the cops!"

"Okay," I said. "Sorry."

The man slammed the door shut.

"Come on," Brit said. "We'd better go."

"Yeah," said Tiffany. "This place gives me the creeps."

"Poor Roberta," Brit said. "What a horrible place to live."

We trooped down the hall, back to the bottom of the steps, and out into the fresh air. We stopped on the sidewalk in front of the apartment.

"What do we do now?" Tiffany asked.

"I don't know what else we can do," I said. "She's either not here, or she doesn't want to talk to us."

"But we can't let the whole night go by and not let her know that we care about her!" Brit said.

"Why don't you call her tonight?" Tiffany said. "Tell her how we feel."

"I can't," Brit said. "She doesn't have a phone. I found that out the other night when I tried to call her about arranging to work on costumes."

"We'll see her tomorrow," I said. "We give our presentation tomorrow, and we can talk to her before social studies class."

"Okay," she said. "I guess that's the only thing we can do."

I looked at Brit, then Tiffany. I saw on their faces just what I was feeling. We'd failed Roberta somehow.

We hunted for Roberta before school on the playground the next day but couldn't find her anywhere.

"I'm glad we're presenting our social studies projects at the beginning of the day," Brit said. "We can get this straightened out with Roberta and get our project over with."

I felt that way too. Besides, I couldn't wait to see the looks on the kids' faces when they saw Roberta in her costume and watched her act.

Mrs. Pettyjohn was standing in the hall outside our classroom when we filed into the building. She caught my eye and waved to me to come over.

"Bring Tiffany and Brit," she said. She looked as if something were wrong.

I hollered to Tiff and Brit, and we followed Mrs. Pettyjohn into the classroom. She closed the door behind us.

"I wanted to talk to you three," she said. "Mrs. Arnstead and I have been trying to get hold of Mrs. Parsley and Roberta since Roberta left school yesterday. Apparently, they don't have a phone."

"I know," said Brit.

"We stopped at her apartment after school," I said. "No one answered the door."

Mrs. Pettyjohn nodded. "Mrs. Arnstead and I drove over yesterday before going home. We had the same experience. Then I returned about eight o'clock. I met Mrs. Parsley." She paused. "Roberta didn't go home when she left here yesterday. I checked again this morning, but Roberta still isn't home."

Brit gasped. "Do you think she's run away?"

"It appears that way," Mrs. Pettyjohn said.

"Did her mother call the police?" I asked.

"Well—actually, Mrs. Arnstead and I did," said Mrs. Pettyjohn.

"So what did Mrs. Parsley say about Roberta?" Tiffany asked.

Mrs. Pettyjohn paused a moment before she spoke. "I think Mrs. Parsley wasn't—feeling too well. I told her that Mrs. Arnstead and I would contact the police for her." She looked around at us. "But I called you in here to say that I think it might be a good idea for the three of you to go ahead and present your skit without Roberta."

"*What!*" we all said together.

"But we can't!" Brit said. "We *need* Roberta! She's an important character in the scene!"

"Could you divide up her lines?" Mrs. Pettyjohn asked.

"But Roberta will probably be back soon," I said. "Can't we just wait for her?"

"I wish we could," Mrs. Pettyjohn said. "But we're at the end of the unit. We'll be starting another unit next week, and we have a film scheduled on Friday. That only leaves tomorrow and Thursday to wait for her."

Brit spoke up. "You really *have* to see Roberta in this skit," she said. "She's so good, and this project will help her grade in social studies."

Mrs. Pettyjohn smiled. "I can see I chose the right people to work with Roberta."

"Don't you think she'll be back soon?" Brit asked.

Mrs. Pettyjohn sighed. "Roberta has a history of running away. One time, she was gone for almost a month."

"A *month!*" we all said at once.

"What did she *do?*" I asked.

"Where did she *go?*" asked Tiffany.

"I don't have all the details," said Mrs. Pettyjohn. "Hopefully, for everybody's sake, she'll be home soon this time. But I think you should plan on giving your skit on Thursday."

"That Hilary!" I said. "She made all this happen!"

"Well, I agree that Hilary was very cruel," said Mrs. Pettyjohn. "But the world is full of people who aren't going to treat us well. Running away never solves anything. It's better to face the problems and try to work them out." She frowned. "You know, when she gets back, she'll need some extra support from you three, in particular." She walked back to the door and opened it. The kids, who'd been waiting in the hall, poured into the classroom.

I turned to Tiffany and Brit. "I sure do hope Roberta gets back by Thursday."

"What if she doesn't?" asked Tiffany.

"Then—" I looked around at all of them, "we'll divide up her lines and give our skit without her." *But please, God, we'd rather not have to do that.*

10

Found!

Roberta didn't come to school the next day. Mrs. Pettyjohn reminded Tiffany, Brit, and me that we should expect to present our skit tomorrow.

"I guess we'd better meet at my house after school to divide up Roberta's lines and practice," I said to Tiff and Brit. They agreed to come.

All day I thought about Roberta. I tried to imagine how she felt when Hilary said those mean things about her mother.

I remembered overhearing Peter Skalen's mother once saying she thought the brownies my mother made for the PTA meeting were dry and tasteless. That made me *SO MAD* to think that anyone would criticize my mother, who'd worked all afternoon on those stupid brownies when she'd had a headache and didn't feel like baking in the first place.

If that made me mad, how would I feel if someone laughed at me in front of other kids and said my mother sat around getting drunk all day—and it was *true?*

I began to understand a little the rage that Roberta must have felt. The rage that came from humiliation, and the helplessness that came from hearing the awful truth about your mother from a mean girl like Hilary.

I wondered if Roberta would show up at school tomorrow. I sure hoped so, but something in the back of my mind told me she wouldn't be there. We'd have to do the skit without her. It just wasn't going to be the same.

Tiff and Brit came over to my house after school and we worked for two hours, dividing Roberta's lines between us. I became the mother in the scene. Our rehearsal was okay, but the skit wasn't as good as when Roberta was with us.

Mom invited Tiff and Brit to stay for supper, and they both agreed. As soon as Dad got home, we all sat down at the table.

"How is the social studies project going without Roberta?" Mom asked after our prayer. She scooped a chicken leg and a big dumpling off the serving tray and put it on Portia's plate.

I shrugged. "It's okay, but it used to be *great.*"

Brit nodded. "If only Roberta would decide to

come back by tomorrow morning," she said. "Everything would be fine."

"What's going to happen to Roberta when she gets back?" Dad asked. "Do you think Hilary will apologize to her?"

"No way," I said. "Hilary's a jerk."

Mom nodded. "You know, when Roberta finally does show up again, she will really need you three kids to stick with her and be her friends."

I suddenly realized that being Roberta's friend really hadn't been all that hard. As long as we treated her kindly, she was okay. Maybe turning the other cheek did work. Jesus' example couldn't be wrong!

"Juliet," my mom said after dinner, "as soon as I have these plates scraped, will you take out the garbage?"

"Sure," I said.

We all helped Mom clear the table. I put on my heavy jacket to go outside. It had turned pretty cold in the last two days, and we could see our breath on the air coming home from school.

"Be right back," I said to Tiff and Brit.

I picked up the garbage and headed out the back door. It was really cold, and I walked quickly back to the garage. The garbage cans were next to the garage on the far side.

I dumped the garbage and set the lid down on the top of the can. Then I started toward the back door. A noise made me stop and look to the back of the yard. I didn't see anything at first. It was cloudy and nearly dark. The playhouse sat in the shadows under the large elm tree.

Did the noise come from the playhouse?

I squinted in the dim light and focused on the one window. I saw a movement inside the little house. Someone was inside.

I knew right away who it was. It had to be.

I ran over to the playhouse and peered in the window. And there she was.

Roberta Parsley sat in the deep shadows of the far corner, her legs drawn up in front of her, shivering in the cold.

11

Roberta's Friends

Roberta!" I blurted out.

Roberta's head jerked up, then she sank back deeper into the shadows. "Great," she mumbled.

I ran around the playhouse and opened the door. She was wearing her light cotton jumper and a light jacket over it that only came to her waist. She must have been freezing.

"Roberta, we were so worried about you," I said. "Do you know that the police are looking for you?"

She leaned forward and her eyes widened in the dim light.

"The *police?*" she said. "Why?"

I realized then that maybe she wondered if the police had tracked her down for shoplifting. I squatted down next to her.

"Because you disappeared," I said. "Everybody's worried about you."

"Did my mother call the police?"

"I think Mrs. Pettyjohn and Mrs. Arnstead did," I said.

Roberta sank back into the corner again. "Oh." She sounded disappointed.

"Roberta," I said, "I'm sorry about what Hilary said to you the other day."

Roberta folded her arms in front of her and cleared her throat. The sound that came out was sort of strangled, and I wondered if she was crying.

"Roberta, it's freezing out here. Aren't you cold?"

She shrugged.

"Have you eaten at all since you left school the other day?"

There was a little pause before she said softly, "No."

"Man, you must be *starving*," I said. "Why don't you come on inside—"

I heard the back door open.

"Hey, Juliet!" yelled Tiffany. "How long does it take to dump the garbage, anyway?"

I walked to the window and saw Tiff and Brit standing on the back porch.

"Hey, you guys," I said, "come on over here."

Roberta groaned. "Why don't you call up the whole class and get them over here? We'll have a party."

"Maybe we'll have to do that," I said, "to convince you that everyone wants you to come back."

"Right," she said.

"They *do!*" I said.

Tiffany and Brit's heads appeared at the window. "Are you nuts, Juliet?" Tiff said. "It's cold out here!"

"We have a visitor," I said and gestured to Roberta in the dark corner.

They both leaned forward and squinted. Brit let out a squeal.

"Roberta! It's you and you're okay! This is *wonderful!* Oh, I'm so glad to see you!"

She and Tiffany ran around to the playhouse door.

"Everyone's going to be happy to see you," Tiffany said to Roberta.

"No, they're not," she said. "Because I'm not coming back."

"Why not?" I asked her.

There was a long pause before she answered. Finally, she shrugged and said, "I hate those guys."

"Which guys?" I asked.

She didn't answer.

"Which guys?" I said again. "Mrs. Pettyjohn?"

"No," Roberta said.

"Mrs. Arnstead?" Brit asked.

"No, not even her," Roberta said.

"Do you hate us?" Brit asked.

"*No*," Roberta said, sounding surprised. "I like you guys."

"We like you too," Brit said.

"Yeah," I said.

There was a short silence.

"So you mean you hate Hilary, right?" I said.

"And those two friends of hers," she said. "I hate them."

"So you're going to let those three girls keep you from going back to school?" I asked her.

"I don't want to see them," Roberta said.

"You sure are giving those three people a lot of power over you," I said.

"What do you mean?" Roberta said.

"There are a lot of kids you like in the class," Brit said.

"And only three that you don't like," I said. "You've decided not to go back to school because of those three dumb people. That's giving them a lot of power over your life." Then I whispered so only Roberta could hear, "And I'm going to tell you about Someone much more powerful." God was answering the prayers I'd been sending His way about Roberta.

Roberta stared at the floor for a long minute.

"I don't know," she said.

"Roberta," I said, "my mother made chicken and dumplings for dinner tonight. . ."

Roberta looked up at me and swallowed. "Chicken and dumplings?"

"Yeah, and boy, was it a good dinner!" Tiffany said.

"And I just happen to know that there's one very large serving left," I said. "Why don't you come inside and eat it, and *then* decide what you're going to do?"

Roberta thought a moment. I couldn't believe she'd need much encouragement. She hadn't eaten in almost two days!

"Okay," she said. She stood up.

"Good!" cried Brit. "You need some nourishment."

Brit took one arm and Tiffany took the other, and they led her out of the playhouse. I followed right behind.

Brit was right; Roberta needed nourishment. But what she needed right now, even more than food, was friends.

And she had them.

12

The Star of the Show

Where's Roberta?" I asked Brit.

Tiffany, Brit, and I were standing in the hall outside our classroom, wearing our pioneer costumes. We were waiting for social studies to begin.

"She's in the bathroom fixing her hair," Brit said. "I told her not to come out until we're ready."

"Oh, hi, Hilary!" I called out over Brit's shoulder.

Hilary, Stacy, and Candy walked down the hall toward us.

Hilary smirked. "So your group is going today, huh?" she said. "Too bad Big Roberta isn't back yet."

Brit opened her mouth to speak, but I jumped in and said, "Yeah, but we're ready."

"Well, we'll be watching!" Hilary said. She turned and walked away.

"Let's surprise everybody," I said to Brit and Tiff.

Mrs. Pettyjohn poked her head out the door. "We're ready to start now. Are you four all set?"

"Yes," I said. "Brit, would you go and tell Roberta to come out now?"

"Right," she said and scooted off.

We hadn't told anyone Roberta was back. She and her mother had come in early to talk to Mrs. Arnstead and Mrs. Pettyjohn.

"How did it go in there?" Brit had asked Roberta after the meeting.

"Okay," Roberta said. "I'm not getting punished or anything. My mom and I have to meet twice a month with Mrs. Pettyjohn and Mrs. Arnstead, and they want Mom to talk to a counselor."

"That's great!" Brit said.

"I can tell Mrs. Pettyjohn likes you," I said.

"Yeah," Roberta said. "She's nice. And so is Mrs. Arnstead."

Tiffany and I walked into the classroom and stood in the back. Mrs. Pettyjohn quieted the class. Then she looked back at us. "Ready?" she asked.

I turned to see Brit and Roberta in the hall; so I motioned for them to come in and nodded to Mrs. Pettyjohn.

All heads in the class turned toward the door. First Brit walked in, and then Roberta. I wish you could have heard it. Complete silence for a long moment. Maybe, at first, the kids didn't realize who that tall, pretty girl was.

Roberta was dressed in her costume with her hair fixed up on her head the way Brit had shown her. Her face had a special glow, and her cheeks were a soft rosy color. She looked sensational.

"*Roberta?*" Stephanie finally said.

"Is that Roberta?" someone else said.

"Roberta," said Mrs. Pettyjohn, "you look *lovely!*"

"Thanks," Roberta whispered.

This time when Roberta accepted the compliment, she didn't look at the floor. She looked right at Mrs. Pettyjohn and smiled.

I glanced at Hilary. She saw me looking at her and scowled, then she crossed her arms across her chest and slumped in her seat.

Tiffany, Brit, Roberta, and I took our places in the front of the room.

"The date is July 20, 1855," I began. "We four women, who made the trip over the Oregon Trail, are getting ready for the barn dance at a neighbor's."

Even though it had been some time since we had all rehearsed together, we remembered our lines perfectly. But it wouldn't have mattered if someone had messed up because no one noticed that anyone other than Roberta was up there.

Roberta was the star of the show. She glowed and smiled. She dazzled everybody with her acting. She played the part of a girl getting ready for a dance, but the excitement inside of the girl in front of the room was for herself, Roberta Parsley.

At the end of the skit, the class broke into thunderous applause. Justin was the first person to stand, then Megan, then Adam and Melissa and Abby and Loretta. Then the whole class was on their feet, clapping. Even Hilary!

And through all of this, Roberta just stood in front of the class with this surprised look on her face.

I leaned over to her and whispered, "I *told* you they wanted you back."

She grinned at me and nodded, and she grinned some more.

All of this happened last year when I was in fifth grade. A year has passed, and I've had a lot of time to think about Roberta and how we tamed her. Mrs. Pettyjohn taught us how to do it. We ignored Roberta when she wasn't nice. But when she *was* nice, we gave her lots of attention and praise and gold apples.

I think this was what Jesus meant about turning the other cheek. He didn't mean you should invite someone to slap you on the other side of

your face. I think He meant that you turn away from an argument and let the angry person say what he wants. You don't have to say anything back.

Roberta's still in our class. Her grades aren't *great*, but they're okay. I think her life with her mother isn't wonderful, so she's still angry sometimes. But she has friends who care about her. I think she feels better about herself now than she used to. I don't think she'll ever run away again— or shoplift.

That reminds me. Just a month after we presented our skit, Roberta got a baby-sitting job with a lady in her apartment. She said she wanted to earn money for some new clothes.

You should see her now. She saves her baby-sitting money and buys clothes that are inexpensive, but they're *in*. She looks great.

And she's happy at school. I can tell because she smiles a lot. Her mom even lets her come to church with us sometimes.

In the Bible Jesus says, "Do everything in love." I like that. I wish everybody lived that way. Jesus' love works miracles.

I should know. I saw a miracle happen when we tamed Roberta Parsley.